THE
INDIANS
AND THE
STRANGERS

THE
INDIANS
AND THE
STRANGERS

Johanna Johnston

Illustrated with woodcuts by
ROCCO NEGRI

DODD, MEAD & COMPANY
New York

CONTENTS

WHO IS
THE STRANGER?

From the earliest times,
the people we call Indians
lived all over the continent of North America,
all over South America,
and on the islands that are nearby.
They were divided into tribes and nations,
and though the people were alike in many ways,
they were different too.
They had different ways of making a living from the land,
different ways of worshipping,
different languages.
They were different enough

7

so that in those times
the people of one tribe or nation were always strangers
to the people of another tribe or nation.

Tribes and nations often fought each other.
They fought for better hunting grounds,
or because of some real or fancied wrong,
or just for the excitement of fighting.
In almost all the tribes and nations
being a brave warrior was the finest thing
that a man could be.
Wars were almost games, or tests of strength,
as they have been for all peoples,
at one time or another.
Few tribes or nations tried to become friendly
with other tribes or nations.
Sometimes they did.
Six great Indian tribes in North America
who spoke the same language
joined to become the Six Iroquois Nations.
But mostly, tribes fought tribes—
enemy against enemy—
stranger against stranger.

And then the *real* strangers came
to the American continents.
These men were quite different in looks
from the bronze-skinned Indians.
They were men who had invented many things
and wanted many things
quite different from anything that the Indians wanted.

There were many surprises,
many cruel things done,
and some kind things too,
when these two different peoples met each other.

This book tells a little about what happened
in some parts of North America
when the Indians whose home it was
met the *real* strangers.

SQUANTO...
and the English
Explorers

When the strangers came ashore
on the Massachusetts coast,
they seemed like some sort of magical beings
to young Squanto
and to everyone else in his village.
Their skin was so pale, their chins so bearded.
They had such curious clothes and weapons.
Above all, they brought such magical gifts—
beads, and mirrors that glittered and flashed,
bright colored cloth,
knives and scissors that cut
like no knives the villagers had ever seen.

11

Squanto was excited, and frightened too,
when the strangers pointed to him
and made it clear, by signs,
that he could have more gifts
if he would get into the little boat
and ride out with them to the great ship
which was anchored farther out in the harbor.
But of course he could not show his fear.
He was no longer a child, but a boy,
almost a man.

So Squanto got into the little boat
and was rowed to the mysterious ship.

On board it, he followed the strangers
down into a dark hold.
There they opened a chest full of treasures
from which he could choose.
But meantime, the sails were being raised,
the anchor was lifted,
and the ship set off to sea.

And so Squanto was kidnapped from his homeland
by some Englishmen who were exploring
the coast of North America.
The Englishmen had no idea of being especially cruel.
They—and the other people of Europe—
had found out only recently that
there were lands across the sea from them.
They dreamed of finding gold, silver, or precious gems
in those lands.
They were not much concerned about the *people*
who lived there
and had lived there for centuries.
They called them Indians
and thought they were ignorant savages.
So they kidnapped the Indian boy

14

as they would have captured a wild animal.
At first, they planned to take him to England with them.
But they stopped at Spain on the way
and there they sold him as a slave.

Now Squanto was in a world very different
from the one he had always known.
It was a world full of pale-skinned, bearded strangers,
a world of houses, buildings, roads
that seemed to cover most of the earth,
a world of animals that he had never seen before—
horses, cows, pigs—
and a thousand other things that were strange—
wheels, wagons, books, glass, guns, clocks.

Then, soon, some men who seemed sorry for Squanto
came and talked with his master
and before long, he was on a ship again.

After a while he was in still another strange country.
Here, too, there were pale-skinned people,
many buildings, strange animals.
And here he lived for a long time

with some people who were kind to him.
The country was England.
and as time passed, Squanto learned to understand
the speech of the people who were kind to him.

One day, because he could speak English,
Squanto found himself once again on a ship.
Some more Englishmen were going to explore
the coast of North America.
They wanted Squanto as a guide and to help them
understand what other Indians said.

The ship crossed the ocean and then
sailed along the American coast
and Squanto was helpful to the Englishmen
just as they had hoped he would be.
They came at last to a part of the coast
that Squanto had known all his life.
Here the captain said,
"We will take you ashore, Squanto.
We have brought you home."
Squanto could hardly believe it.
But then came something even harder to believe.

16

When the Englishmen rowed him ashore,
they found that nobody was living in the village
that he had known as a boy.
What had happened? Where was everybody?

The Englishmen tried to understand it also.
"Perhaps there was a great sickness and many died,"
one said, "and the others went to join another tribe."
And then, as Squanto looked around him,
the Englishmen said, "Come. We will go back to the ship
and sail on until we come to another village.
Perhaps you will find some of your family there."

And so it was that Squanto finally came
to Pokanoket, the home of Massasoit,
chief of the Wampanoags,
and was welcomed by the people there.
He said good-bye to the Englishmen
and watched them sail away.

He did not think of the white men as magical beings now.
They had many things that his own people did not, yes—
but he had seen for himself that

17

they ate, slept, laughed, cried, hurt themselves
or hurt others,
just like his own people.
Some were cruel or thoughtless,
but others were kind.
Some had kidnapped him, but
others had treated him well
and finally brought him home again.

Now, as Squanto roamed the forests, hunting the deer,
or watched the stars or clouds,
or sat with the others around the fires at night,
he remembered many of the white strangers kindly,
and wondered if any of them
would visit his land again.

POWHATAN...
and the Settlers
at Jamestown

"Kneel, Powhatan, and bow your head,"
said Captain John Smith.
He held forward a beautiful crown
as he stood before the tall, old chief.
Jewels in the crown sparkled in the sun.
"Kneel," said the captain.
But Powhatan only stood and stared at the white man.
He knew very well what the captain was saying.
He had been acquainted with white men
for almost two years now,
ever since a party of Englishmen had landed
at the mouth of the river

21

and started a settlement there, on Powhatan's territory.
He had learned their language.

He had learned other things about them too.
He did not think they were magical beings at all.
It was true that they had guns
which seemed very much like magical weapons,
and Powhatan wished that he and his people
could get more of them from the white men.
But the white men did not like to trade guns.
They were the one powerful thing they had.
Without them, they were almost helpless.
They did not know how to plant,
how to hunt, or how to find their way through the forest.

And now, here was Captain Smith offering him a crown
which had come from across the sea.
"King James had it made especially for you,"
Captain Smith said.
Powhatan looked at the crown.
He had been pleased by such glittering gifts
when the white men first came,
but now he knew that gifts generally meant

the white men hoped to get more land
from Powhatan's people.
And once they had decided some land was theirs,
they did not want anyone else to set foot on it,
even to hunt.
Powhatan thought they were very ignorant
not to know that land was meant for *everyone* to use.

"Kneel down," Captain Smith said again.
"You have to go down on your knees and bow your head
for me to put the crown on."

"Have to?" thought Powhatan. "*Have* to?"
Suddenly, he was remembering the time a year before
when Captain John Smith had stood before him
as a prisoner.
Powhatan's braves had captured Smith in the forest
and all of them had gathered around Powhatan then
and shouted that Smith must die.
Three of Powhatan's people had been killed
by white men who had been with Smith.
It was only right that Smith be killed in return.
But Powhatan's young daughter, Pocahontas,

had cried out, begging that the white man be spared.
And Powhatan had granted her wish.
He had saved John Smith's life.
Now the man he had saved was telling him, Powhatan,
that he had to go down on his knees,
as if he were pleading for something.

Once again, hundreds of his braves were gathered around.
Dozens of the women and children of the village
were there also, waiting to see what he would do.

Captain Smith was still talking.
"King James wants you to know his friendship.
That is why he is making you Emperor of the Indies."

Suddenly Powhatan lost patience.
How did some white chief across the water
think that he could make Powhatan emperor of anything?
Powhatan had won his own honors.
Through the years he had fought
with the tribes around about and defeated them,
and then made a good peace with each of them.
Now he was chief of more than thirty tribes.

24

"No!" Powhatan was speaking at last.
"No, I will not kneel. I am king here
and I kneel for no one."

"Aiieee!" cried the braves around Powhatan, proudly.
Captain Smith looked surprised.
He had thought Powhatan would be pleased
to have the King of England send him a crown.
He stepped forward quickly, reached up,
and put the crown on Powhatan's head.
"There," he said. "You are Emperor of the Indies."
Powhatan glared.
For a moment, everyone held his breath.
Would Powhatan feel that he had been insulted?
Would he take the crown off and fling it down?
And if he did, then what?

Then Powhatan spoke, quietly.
"I am Powhatan, chief of the Powhatan Union.
As chief, I accept the gift of my brother across the sea.
If he should ever cross the water to visit me,
I will give him a crown in return.
Now, let us go to the feast."

25

Then everyone relaxed.
There was not going to be any trouble, after all.
The women hurried to the fires to get the bowls of food.
The children danced and ran about.
Side by side, Powhatan and the captain
walked to the feasting area.

Who had won?
Captain Smith hoped that he had,
and that since Powhatan was wearing the crown
he was promising that he and his people
would always be friendly with the English settlers.

But Powhatan was sure that he had won.
He had not bent his knee nor bowed his head.
He was chief in his own land and had promised nothing.
He would behave toward the strangers
as seemed right to him.
He would be friendly so long as they deserved friendship,
but if they broke their promises
or hurt his people,
then he would not be friendly.
And that was how it was in the Virginia colony
so long as Powhatan lived.

27

MASSASOIT...
and the Pilgrims

Massasoit, chief of the Wampanoags,
took a small bit of meat from the kettle,
held it up toward the sky,
and then threw it into the fire under the kettle.
Then he saw that
all the English men, women, and children
were staring at him.
"Why did you do that?" asked Edward Winslow,
one of the chief men of the little white settlement
that the English called Plymouth.
Massasoit answered. "I thank the Great Spirit

29

for the good gifts of the land.
I give back a bit to show my thanks."

Edward Winslow smiled and then shook his head.
"That is not the way to thank the true God," he said.
"We will teach you how to worship that God."
Then Winslow folded his hands and bowed his head.
All the English men, women, and children did the same.
Then one of the men began to pray.

Massasoit and the braves who were with him
watched and listened.
Massasoit's dark, handsome face showed nothing,
but he was not happy with what Winslow had said.
Winslow had no right to speak as though
the Great Spirit were not true.
The Great Spirit was at the heart and center of everything—
earth, sun, water, animals, people, the whole world.
Indians had believed so for centuries.
If the white men wanted to believe something else,
Massasoit would say nothing.
That was their business.
But the white men should show Indians the same politeness.

30

The white man's prayer came to an end at last.
It was time for the feast.
The English women passed the great bowls of food.
Everyone began eating, talking, and laughing.
It was a happy time of celebrating
a good harvest and food laid by for the winter.

Massasoit tried to forget his troubling thoughts.
He wanted these white men as his friends.
All through the summer, he and his people had helped them.
One of his men, Squanto, who knew English
because he had been kidnapped to England for a time,
had been happy to stay with the Pilgrims,
showing them how to plant corn and how to hunt and fish.
In return, Massasoit hoped that the white men,
with their guns,
would help him and his people,
if their old enemies, the Narragansetts, should attack them.

But he also hoped that there would be no more talk
about the white man's God.
He knew that he would not give up his belief
in the Great Spirit to keep their friendship.

31

After the feast, Massasoit and his braves left to return to
their home in Pokanoket.
And then, not many months after that,
Massasoit became sick.
He grew worse and worse.
The medicine men of his tribe and the wise old women
tried all their remedies—in vain.
At last a messenger was sent to tell the men at Plymouth
that Massasoit was dying.

Edward Winslow came back with the messenger
to Pokanoket.
He did not have any special medicines with him—
only some syrups and jellies.
He fed these to Massasoit and
Massasoit began to get better.
Perhaps he was about to get better anyway,
but it did not seem that way to him.
Massasoit was sure that Winslow had saved his life.
He took Winslow's hand and said,
"Now I see the English are my friends and love me,
and whilst I live
I will never forget this kindness they have showed me."

32

Edward Winslow was happy that
Massasoit was going to get well.
"You are still young," he told the chief.
"There is much you can do for your people.
You can learn about the true God and accept him
and get your people to do so too.
Forget these stories about a Great Spirit
who lives in trees and animals
as well as the souls of men.
Accept the true God."

Massasoit closed his eyes. What could he say?
Winslow *was* his friend now, beyond any going back on it.
But he wondered.
"Why do they think their ways are the only true ways?
They know many things that we do not—that is plain.
But we know our ways, and what is good for us.
Why must they want every man to follow their pattern?"
Massasoit was friendly and helpful to the English
all his life long—
but he still kept wondering.

PHILIP...
and the New England Colonists

"They took our men to their court?
They sentenced them to death and then killed them?
Do they forget we have our own laws
and our own justice?"
It was Philip speaking.
Philip, the second son of Massasoit,
was now chief of the Wampanoags.
He sat on a hillside near one of the longhouses
at Pokanoket.
Around him were the braves who had brought the news,
all of them looking angry.

35

Much had changed since the days when
Massasoit and the Pilgrims had been friends.
Many, many more white people had come to America.
Their farms covered miles of land along the coast
and far inland as well, and they wanted no Indians
anywhere on what they called *their* land.
Here and there, Indians and white men had fought.
White men and Indians alike had been killed.
And then had come a war
when the men of the new English colonies—
Massachusetts, Plymouth Bay, and Connecticut—
had joined together to punish the people of the Pequot tribe
for the killing of a white man.

Philip could remember that war.
He remembered how the white soldiers
had burned Pequot forts,
killing hundreds of men, women, and children,
and then how they had followed and killed
the few who survived.

Perhaps it was then that Philip began
to have different feelings than his father had

about the white strangers.
Perhaps it was then that he began to fear
and hate them.
Philip thought they wanted to take away everything
from the Indians.
They wanted to take
their hunting grounds, their freedom to roam,
their customs, their beliefs.
And now, he had this latest news.
The white men of Plymouth had stepped into
the middle of an Indian quarrel.
They had arrested and punished some Indians
whom *they* thought were guilty.

"So!" cried one of the braves, jumping to his feet.
"We have suffered enough.
Now we go on the warpath."
The other braves jumped to their feet also.
"Yes," they cried. "It is time."

But Philip was on his feet as well.
"No!" he said. "We do not attack now."
The plan is not ready."

37

"Oh, the plan—the plan," cried the braves angrily.
"Yes, the plan," said Philip.
For the truth was that Philip had been working secretly
for years, trying
to get all the Indian tribes of the northeast
to agree to fight together
in one great war against the strangers,
to force them to go back across the sea
where they came from.

"We cannot wait for the plan," said one brave.
"Who will join us anyway?" said another.
"And who wants them?" said still another.
"Come! To the warpath now."
He picked up his bow from the ground
and began to test the string.
"Hieee! Hieee!" yelled the others.

"Listen to me," said Philip.
"Our only chance is to strike together,
the way the white men do.
Perhaps we must strike sooner than I thought,
but we must at least send the black wampum belt

to all the chiefs who have promised to join us
when I send the word.
Come! Who will carry the wampum to the Narragansetts?"

"There is no time for that," one brave said.
"No, no time," said another.
"Come, let us sharpen our arrows,
put on our war paint, and strike."
And then the braves were running to the longhouses,
shouting the war cry to other braves
who also began to whoop and run for their arrows.

Philip stood on the hillside, looking after them unhappily.
He had hoped for another year at least
to win more tribes as allies.
Was his whole plan to be ruined now
because his men would not wait?
Then he lifted his head
and looked at the sky.
"All right," he thought.
"We go on the warpath.
But all will not be lost.
We will strike and strike—and strike again.

And it will be as I told the English

when I reminded them of how my father had fed them

and helped them when they were few and hungry.

I told them that there are too many of them now

and they take more land every day.

But I will not live to be without a country."

The history books tell of the war that followed—

King Philip's War, it was called.

The Indians did strike and strike and strike again,

and they filled the white men with terror.

Philip was a brilliant warrior, and perhaps,

if his men *had* been willing to wait

until his plan was ready,

they might have won the war.

As it was, the white men did unite.

They came from all the northern colonies

to track Philip and his men from spot to spot.

And so, in the end, the Indians lost the war,

and Philip himself was killed near his home, Pokanoket.

He had said he would not live to be without a country

and that was how it was.

41

TAMMANY...
and the Quakers

The tribes who lived in the forests and meadows
along the great river now known as the Delaware
were a happy, wandering people
who called themselves the Leni-Lenapes,
which meant "the real people."
Indeed, there was reason for them to think that
they *were* the real people.
They had fine hunting in their forests.
They could grow crops easily in their meadows.
They had few enemies.
And they had a wise and thoughtful chief,

43

named Tamenend, or Tammany, *chief*
who was more interested in helping his people
to a better life than in making war.

But now white people were coming from England
to build a city on the banks of the great river.
"We want you to know that we come in peace,"
said the Englishman, Captain Markham,
who had arrived before the others.
He sat with Tammany by the chief's wigwam
in the summer village near the river.
This, in itself, was something new—
a white man coming first to the Indians
to ask if it was all right.
"You see," Captain Markham went on,
"We are a people who do not believe in war.
We are Quakers."

"Quakers?" said Tammany.
It was a strange word.
"The name we have for ourselves," Markham said,
"is Friends.
Our leader, who brings us here to make new lives in America,

is <u>William Penn</u>. *leader*
You will find he *is* a friend, Tammany."

Tammany was silent a moment, as was polite.
Then he said, "It sounds well.
I await the meeting with your chief, William Penn."
He <u>took</u> a coal from the fire nearby and <u>lit the pipe</u>
he was holding.
He took a puff, and then passed the pipe to Captain Markham
who also took a puff.
<u>It was the Indian way of showing it had been</u>
<u>a good meeting.</u>

William Penn and his party were not due to come
until the next summer.
Tammany had all winter to wonder
if everything would be as the captain had promised.
But he had known white men before—
men from Holland and men from Sweden—
who had set up trading posts down the river.
The Leni-Lenapes had always found them friendly
and fair in their trade for furs.
Why should he expect trouble?

45

On a bright day of summer, the ship came up the river.
Some of the "real people"—the Leni-Lenapes—
were watching as the party of Friends came ashore.
They saw one man who must be the leader, William Penn.
Everyone seemed to go to him for advice.

In the next days, the Leni-Lenapes watched
as men cut down trees, hewed logs,
and built shelters on the land by the river.
But soon word went out to Tammany,
and the other chiefs of the Leni-Lenapes,
that William Penn wanted to meet with them.
He asked that they meet under a large elm by the river,
a tree so big and old that everyone knew it.

Tammany and the other chiefs—and hundreds of their braves
and their women and children as well—
came to the meeting.
Most of the men and many of the women and children
from Penn's city were there also.
William Penn met with Tammany and the other chiefs
under the great elm.
He said all that Captain Markham had promised.

47

And there was something about him
that made the chiefs believe his words.
"We will never do any wrong to you or your people.
We will live in love with you
so long as the sun gives light."

The chiefs nodded when he had finished.
Then Tammany rose to speak.
"If we make the treaty with you and
smoke the pipe of peace together,
you will be our brothers," he said.
He brought forth the pipe, took a puff,
and passed it to William Penn.
Penn puffed it and passed it to another chief,
and so it went around the circle.

Penn gave a signal and some of his men
brought forward big chests and put them before the chiefs.
Here was the payment for the Indian land
that Penn and his people were taking.
The chests were opened and the Indians saw
beads, mirrors, jewelry, knives, scissors,
pots, pans, tools, shawls, coats, hats, and
hundreds of other things.

Perhaps they were not worth a great deal to the white men,
but Tammany and the other chiefs were pleased.

The treaty was signed. The business part was over.
The Indian women had brought
pots of venison and succotash.
The Quaker women had brought food also.
Everyone ate until he could hold no more.
Then the games began—games of running and jumping
at which the Leni-Lenapes were very good.
William Penn took off his fancy coat
and lined up with the braves who were starting
another race.
Soon everyone was astonished.
Penn, their new brother, could run as fast
as the fastest brave.

When the shadows began to fall,
Friends and Leni-Lenapes smiled at each other
as they parted to go home.
Tammany went back to his wigwam well content.
It seemed to him that the "real people" and
the people who called themselves Friends
could live together in peace.

He was right.

The trust and friendship

begun that day under the great elm lasted for many years.

The city of Philadelphia which William Penn started

grew and prospered

and the "real people" were welcome there.

The Friends did not try to change their beliefs.

To them, every man's religion was his own concern.

As they needed more land, they paid fair prices for it,

and it seemed there was still plenty of land.

It was a good time.

PONTIAC...
and the French

"Yes, I fear it is over, *mon ami*," said the Frenchman
who ran the trading post. He sighed.
"The good hunting and trapping, the fine fur trade—finished.
The English are coming to take over the fort.
The English are coming to clear the land for farms.
We know how it is when the English come."

The tall chief across the counter from the trader
had a stern look on his face.
"I will not let it happen," he said.

51

The Frenchman looked at him and smiled sadly.
"Pontiac," he said,
"you are a brave chief, a great warrior—
and a stubborn man.
But what is done is done. Accept it."

This was impossible for Pontiac, a chief of the Ottawas.
All his life he had known Frenchmen as good neighbors,
for he lived in that northern and western part of America
where Frenchmen rather than Englishmen had come.
And the French there had acted differently in America
from the English.
They were interested in the furs
that they could buy from the Indians
and send back to France for a good profit.
So they had set up trading posts and forts
along the northern rivers and around the Great Lakes.
They hunted with the Indians, trapped with them,
and married Indian women.

But the English in America began to be fearful
of the French who were there.
They found reasons to make war against them.

53

Many of the northern Indians were glad to fight
along with the French in this war.
Pontiac had led his Ottawas in battle to help the French,
and at first they had some fine victories.
But then, in the end, the French were defeated.
Soon English soldiers would be taking over Fort Detroit
from the French.
An English trader would take over the trading post.

"I will not let it happen," Pontiac had said.
But he was not just being stubborn.
He had a plan.
A plan to unite all the tribes along the rivers and lakes
and then arrange for them to strike
at the forts the English were taking from the French—
all at the same time.
And then, after he had struck terror
up and down the English line,
Pontiac was sure the French would join him.
Together they would fight the English again,
and this time, they would drive them away.

Everything went smoothly for Pontiac.

Within two years, dozens of chiefs agreed to join him
and to strike when he sent the word.
When the day came that Pontiac had chosen,
thousands of warriors swooped out of the forests
along the English frontier,
and howled down on forts and blockhouses.
Hundreds of white people were killed.
Ten forts were taken.
Pontiac's War began just as he planned.

Only three forts managed to hold out.
One was Fort Detroit, the one nearest Pontiac's home.
Pontiac had intended to lead the attack on that one himself.
but the soldiers heard of the planned surprise.
They barricaded themselves inside the fort.

Now Pontiac showed that he was indeed a stubborn man.
He decided to keep the fort under siege.
This meant watching it night and day
so that no one inside could get out
and no help or food from outside could get in.
It was not the Indian way of fighting.
The Indian way was to make a quick attack

and then disappear into the forest.
That was what the braves who were with Pontiac
wanted to do now.

Day after day, Pontiac went among his warriors.
"Supplies will be coming to the English
down the river," he said.
"We can fire on them and dump the supplies.
Other English soldiers will be coming to their relief.
We can fight them. If we stay long enough,
the French will come to help us."

Supplies did come down the river, as Pontiac had said,
and he and his men sank the boats.
English soldiers did try to come to the relief
of the soldiers in the fort
and Pontiac and his men held them off.
But the French did *not* come to help Pontiac and his men.

Day after day, week after week, Pontiac kept his men
camped near the fort.
But then bad news came from here, there, and everywhere.
Other tribes who had joined him had given up.

Indians had been badly defeated in the north.
Finally, after more than five months,
Pontiac could no longer hold his braves
to the siege of Fort Detroit.
He let them go.

But he still could not believe that the French
would not come to his aid.
He went here and there, looking for French officers.
Finally, he found one who convinced him of the truth.
France had signed a peace treaty with England.
Frenchmen would no longer
fight Englishmen in America.

After that, Pontiac gave up too.
When the English sent some men
to talk peace with him,
he listened quietly.
Then he took the eagle feather from his hair
and said, "Pontiac is no longer a warrior.
Pontiac is now a hunter.
He goes on lonely trails in the forest.
He keeps the peace with his white brother."

57

That was the end of Pontiac's War.
For a long time, the English in America remembered it
with horror.
But as the years passed,
they finally realized what a great warrior Pontiac had been,
a clever man who had united dozens of tribes,
a brave man who had fought for his own way of life,
and a stubborn man
who had managed to hold Fort Detroit in a state of siege
for over half a year.

JOSEPH BRANT...
and the English

"His Majesty will see you now," said the servant,
and he turned to lead the way through the great hall,
to the special room where King George III
received visitors.
Joseph Brant, a chief of the Mohawks,
dressed in white men's clothing for the occasion,
followed the servant,
thinking of what he would say to England's king.

Once again, Indians were having to choose
between different groups of white people in America.

59

This time the choice was between those Englishmen
who were loyal to England's king
and the English, Dutch, Swedes, Germans,
and other Europeans in America
who had begun to think of themselves as *Americans*.
Those who called themselves Americans
were unhappy with laws passed for them in England.
They had declared that they wanted to be independent
of England and have a new nation in America.

Most Indians could see little difference between
the two groups.
Both the loyal English and the Americans
took Indian land and spoiled it as hunting ground.
When the fighting began between Americans and English,
many Indians were ready to join in,
not caring which side they were on.
But the English wanted the Indians to be loyal to them.
The Americans wanted the Indians on their side.

Joseph Brant, whose Indian named was Thayandanegea,
had chosen which side he was on right away.
As a boy, he had lived in the home of Sir William Johnson,

a kind and wealthy Englishman, who had come
to the New York colony in America,
to handle dealings with the Indians there.
Sir William had treated Joseph like a son
but he had never asked him to forget
that first of all he was an Indian.
So Joseph went to school and learned to read and write.
But he had also gone on the warpath with the Mohawks.
He went to their councils, and spoke for them
with the white men, and finally,
when he was in his twenties, he had been chosen chief
of the Mohawk nation.

Then came the quarrel between
the English and the Americans.
Whose side was Joseph Brant on?
He was on the side that Sir William would have been on,
were he still alive.
He was for England and the king.

And now, here he was in London,
to talk with the King himself
about the part that the Mohawks might play in the war.

"Mohawks, Senecas, Cayugas,
Onondagas, Oneidas, Tuscaroras—
those are the Six Nations of the Iroquois,"
Joseph Brant told the King.
"If all the nations were to help the English,
you would have powerful aid."
The King nodded, and asked, "But will they help?"
Joseph Brant said, "Much land has been taken
from the Iroquois unfairly.
If *you* will promise a return of that land,
I think *I* can promise *you* the loyalty
of the Six Nations."
The King looked pleased. "Very well, Joseph Brant,"
he said. "I will depend on you, and when the war is won,
you may depend on me to return the land."

Soon Joseph Brant was on his way back to America.
He wondered if he had made too big a promise.
But when he came to New York
he saw that the English had captured that city
and the Americans were in retreat.
This seemed proof that the English were going to win.
And so it would be easy

to bring the Six Nations to the English side.
He set off for the Iroquois lands in northern New York
full of hope.

He could hardly believe it when the Onondagas,
who kept the council fire for the Six Nations,
were very slow in agreeing to help the English,
no matter what promises the English had made.
Then the Tuscaroras and the Oneidas also refused.
They listened to him argue that the Six Nations
should fight together in any case.
Then they reminded him that when Pontiac of the Ottawas
had wanted to unite all Indians years before,
he had been *against* union then.

Joseph Brant began to wonder about the choices
he had made in his life.
Should he have joined Pontiac long ago,
even though Pontiac had been against the English?
It was too late to wonder now.
He went on from nation to nation, and at last,
his own Mohawks, the Senecas, and the Cayugas
agreed to fight for the English.

64

Now Joseph Brant put on war paint
and led the Iroquois who joined him
against the Americans.
Some of the battles were terrible.
The Americans came to fear and hate the name of Brant.

And then—the war was over.
The Americans had won. Not the English.
Joseph Brant had chosen the wrong side, it seemed.

What good now was the King's promise
that he would return their land to the Iroquois?
The Iroquois would be lucky if the Americans
did not take all the rest of their land from them.

Fortunately, George Washington, the American leader,
was a just and generous man.
He did not want the Iroquois punished.
He arranged that they should keep much of their land
in New York.
Later, the English, who still held Canada,
showed their thanks to Joseph Brant
by giving him some land there.

But in the years that followed,

when Joseph Brant thought about the choices he had made,

he thought that it hardly mattered

if Indians chose Americans, English, or—

as in Pontiac's time—the French.

The most important thing was for Indians to act together.

For the rest of his life, he worked and traveled

and talked to the tribes,

urging them to do just that.

SACAJAWEA...
and Lewis and Clark

Was it possible?

Was she really going to see the Shining Mountains again?

Sacajawea could hardly believe it.

She had been a child when the Hidatsa people

carried her away from the mountain country

after a fight with her own people, the Shoshoni.

Through the years, the wandering Hidatsa had taken her

farther and farther east, miles to the east.

She was a young woman now,

married to a French-Canadian trapper, named Charbonneau.

It was he, her husband, who was saying that

she would see the mountains again.
And he told her how and why.

A group of Americans from even farther to the east
had come to Fort Mandan,
where Sacajawea and her husband lived.
The Americans were going west—
west as far as the land went—
and they wanted a guide.
Sacajawea's husband had said that he and his wife
would take the job.
Two young captains, Captain Lewis and Captain Clark,
were leading the group.
They wondered if Sacajawea should come too.
"She is a woman—very young.
Our journey is going to be a hard one," they said.
But Sacajawea's husband replied, "She is strong.
Besides, she is a Shoshoni,
and you know that the Shoshoni are one of the western tribes
who have horses.
She will help you get horses from them
to travel over the mountains."
And so it was settled.

68

Sacajawea would go with her husband, Charbonneau,
on the long journey with Lewis and Clark.
With her also would go her baby boy,
who had been born while Charbonneau
was arranging the trip.

When spring came, the group set off in dugout canoes,
to follow the Missouri River westward.
Sacajawea sat in one of the canoes,
with her baby on her back in a cradleboard.
Secretly, she wondered what kind of journey
the Americans were making.
Her husband had told her that the Americans had bought
many miles of the country from France
and these men just wanted to explore it.
But Sacajawea saw that they had many guns with them.
If she helped lead them to her people,
would they do the Shoshoni harm?
Day after day, they traveled,
and Sacajawea watched and listened.

Every night, the two captains wrote in journals,
making notes on what they had seen that day,

for this country had never been seen by white men before.
If Sacajawea had seen something interesting,
or brought them a flower or a rock,
they wrote about that too.

Every day there was a new adventure.
Once some of the men were frightened by a grizzly bear.
One day there was a storm and the main canoe
almost turned over.
Papers, maps and captains' journals
floated off into the water.
Sacajawea jumped into the water and swam about
collecting the papers.
The captains were very grateful to her.
And Sacajawea was happy that she had been able to help.
She had begun to like and trust the Americans.

The river narrowed and the hills grew higher.
Sometimes they had to leave the water
and climb on land, carrying the canoes.
Higher they went, and higher, until at last,
they came to a pass.

71

Ahead they saw the snowy peaks of the Rocky Mountains—
Sacajawea's Shining Mountains.

Sacajawea stood very still, just looking.
Then she took her baby from her back
and held him so that he could see the mountains too.
They were very near Shoshoni country now.
Sacajawea taught the captains some Shoshoni words
and friendly signs to help them
when they met her people.
And she wondered if anyone who had known her
when she was a little girl would still be with the tribe.
She was sure her older brother had been killed
in the long-ago attack when she had been stolen away.

The day came when they met the Shoshoni,
galloping up on the horses that were their pride.
Years before, Spaniards had brought horses to Mexico,
and some had escaped to the plains and become wild.
The Shoshoni, like other western Indians,
had caught some and tamed them.
Now they could not think how they had hunted buffalo
without horses.

Captain Lewis and Captain Clark greeted the Shoshoni chief
with the words Sacajawea had taught them.
Then they called Sacajawea to tell them
what the chief was saying.
Sacajawea came and looked up at the chief—
and could hardly believe what she saw.
The chief was her own brother.
"Little Bear!" she cried.
"Sacajawea—Bird Girl!" he said.

Now, with Sacajawea's help, it was easy for the Americans
to borrow horses from the Shoshoni
for the journey over the Rocky Mountains.
And the journey went on.
Up, up, up, they went, to what seemed the top of the world.
And then down again,
and then across more miles to find the Columbia River.
Here they left the horses and took to boats again.
Then they traveled more miles, past rapids and rocks,
until, on a day of blowing rain and fog,
they saw ahead the waters of the Pacific Ocean.
For the first time white men had crossed
the whole continent of America.

73

Surely it was also the first time that
an Indian girl had crossed half a continent
to stand beside an ocean
so far from where she had been born.

They spent the winter by the ocean.
In the spring they began the long journey home.
When they got back to Fort Mandan,
it was time for Sacajawea
and her husband to say good-bye to the Americans.
Sacajawea was sad as she parted from the captains.
Many white people had brought fear and trouble
to the Indian people in the past.
Many more would do so in the future.
But Sacajawea had known something better—
a wonderful journey and strangers who had become friends.

75

TECUMSEH...
and the Ohio
Settlers

Tecumseh, chief of the Shawnees, sat on one end
of a bench.
The white man sat on the other end.
They were having a talk—or powwow—
about the land that the white men were taking
from the Indians who lived in the rich Ohio Valley.
As Tecumseh talked, he moved closer to the white man,
who was William Henry Harrison,
governor of the new state of Indiana.
Tecumseh moved closer—and closer still.
Finally Harrison looked at Tecumseh in surprise.
"You are pushing me off the bench, Tecumseh," he said.

"Ah," said Tecumseh, and he laughed, but not happily.
"Now you may know a little of how we Indians feel
as the white men push us from our land."

The governor looked away, not sure what to say.
It was like Tecumseh to make his point
in such a simple, easy way.
Tecumseh was a man who saw things clearly
and spoke of what he saw with power.
The governor, who was also a soldier,
wondered how he was going to win the lands
of the Middle West from Tecumseh and his people.

"Sell a country?" Tecumseh had cried the day before,
when the powwow began.
"Why not sell the air;
the clouds and the great sea as well as the earth?
Did not the Great Spirit make them all
for the use of his children?"

Governor Harrison knew that
Tecumseh was making speeches like that
to tribes up and down the Ohio River.

He was filling them with excitement,
telling them that they must work and fight
for a great *Indian* state
where only Indians would live
and the white man could not come.
Tecumseh was going farther.
He was visiting the tribes that lived along the Mississippi,
and winning them to the same idea
of an Indian state.
It was an idea that Indians had been slow to accept before,
but when Tecumseh spoke,
they suddenly saw it as good and possible.

Harrison was frightened when he thought
of the Indians uniting in this way.
But what could he do?
The powwow with Tecumseh went on for another day,
but nothing was settled.
Tecumseh went on his way again,
to make more speeches urging the Indians to unite.

Now Harrison thought about Tecumseh's brother,
who also spoke with a golden tongue.

People called him the Prophet,
because he preached that good days would come again
for the Indians
when they gave up all white men's ways,
stopped drinking whiskey,
and returned to the worship of the Great Spirit.
The Prophet did not travel as Tecumseh did.
He had settled in a village on the banks of
a little river called the Tippecanoe.
Many hundreds of Indians gathered about him there.
A thousand and more of Tecumseh's warriors
stayed there also, waiting for the day
when Tecumseh would say it was time to strike.

Harrison decided that he would march against that village
while Tecumseh was away.
He gathered a number of troops and set forth.
Tecumseh had long since made his brother promise
not to fight—until the time was right.
But when the braves at Tippecanoe
saw the white men camped across the river,
the Prophet would not keep them from making
a surprise attack during the night.

81

Once again, it was a fight that happened too soon.
The Indians were defeated.
Harrison led his Americans into the Indian village
to burn and destroy everything there.

When Tecumseh came back from his travelings
the town was in ruins.
And so, it seemed, were his hopes for uniting the tribes
in one great effort to win an Indian state.

Still, Tecumseh did not give up fighting
for his country and his people.
When the War of 1812 began
between the English and the Americans
Tecumseh led his people against the Americans,
hoping that if the English won
they would grant the Indians' wish
for a state of their own.
In that war, Tecumseh was killed,
believing to the end that
no one could sell a country,
any more than the air or the sea.

BLACK HAWK...
and the Illinois Settlers

"Go ahead. Clear the land. Start planting,"
Black Hawk said.
The people he had led to the land
looked around uneasily.
Not far away, white men were already plowing
and planting in fields that had always belonged
to Black Hawk's people—the Sacs.

Why were the white people there?
Because Keokuk, a chief of the Fox tribe,
had signed a treaty with the white men,

promising that the Indians who lived on
the eastern side of the Mississippi River
would move across the river to the west.
Black Hawk was very angry when he heard about the treaty.
The Sacs and the Fox had always been friends
and fought and traveled together.
But this had not given Keokuk the right
to sell away the land where Black Hawk's people
had always farmed, while Black Hawk was away hunting.
"Plow!" Black Hawk said now. "Plant."
And the people began to do so.

But when the white men
who had come onto the Sacs' land
saw Black Hawk and his people on the land nearby,
they banded together and marched against them.
Black Hawk had not brought many braves with him.
Soon he and his people were forced
back across the Mississippi River to the west.

All the next winter, instead of hunting,
Black Hawk was winning braves to come with him

and fight for the Sacs' farming land
on the eastern side of the river.
In the spring they came across the river—
by the hundreds—
and they swooped down on the little farms and settlements
that the white people had started.

The war called Black Hawk's War had begun.
While it lasted, Black Hawk and his men spread terror
through all the Illinois country.
They burned, they looted, they took scalps.
Why not? This was their country
that another chief had sold to the white men
without their consent.

But soon white men were coming from everywhere.
In battle after battle, Black Hawk and his braves
were pressed back.
They were pushed to the banks of the Mississippi River.
Then, as a hundred and more of his men
dived into the river to swim across it to safety,
Black Hawk mounted his pony
and fled to the north.

Black Hawk's War was over.

Soon Black Hawk himself was a prisoner of the white men.

They allowed him to make a speech to his people.

"Black Hawk is an Indian," he said.

"He has done nothing of which an Indian need be ashamed.

He has fought the battles of his country

against the white men

who came year after year to cheat them...

Black Hawk is satisfied.

He will go to the world of spirits contented.

Farewell to my nation!

Farewell to Black Hawk."

But it was not really farewell to Black Hawk, yet.

He was not kept in prison long.

After he was let out, he made a kind of peace

with the white men,

and with his old enemy, Keokuk, too.

Keokuk's quiet way of thinking and speaking

had caused the white men to promise the Sacs and the Fox

large tracts of good land west of the Mississippi.

If the white men kept their promise

not to try to take this land too,

Black Hawk's people could go on in the old way,
hunting in the winter, farming in the summer.

So Black Hawk smoked the pipe of peace with Keokuk,
and moved quietly among the white men,
no longer frightening them with his gun or tomahawk.
But still, it seemed to him,
he had said farewell to his nation.

SEQUOYA...
and the White
Men's Writing

"Make that sound again," Sequoya said
to a friend who sat under a tree near his work bench.
"Tqua," said the friend.
"Yes," said Sequoya, nodding.
He took a quill and drew a little design
on the birch bark he held in his other hand.
Then he picked up another piece of birch bark
and compared the design on the one
with the design on the other.
The friend leaned over to look also.
Then he shook his head.

89

"I think you had better give up this foolishness, Sequoya,
and spend more time making those silver buckles
that the white men like so well."

But Sequoya did not think he was doing anything foolish.
The white men could make marks on paper and
send messages to each other across long distances.
The messages told much more than the wampum belts
which could only carry one word of meaning
like "war" or "peace."
The white men's messages seemed like "talking leaves"
to Sequoya.
From the first time he saw them, he thought
how wonderful it would be if his people
could talk to each other that way.

Sequoya's people were the Cherokees,
one of five great tribes that lived in the southeastern part
of the United States
(what is now Tennessee, Alabama, and Georgia.)
White men called them the "Five Civilized Tribes"
because they had been so quick to learn
the ways of white men that were useful to them.

But for all that they learned about new ways of farming,
they had no way to write down the Cherokee language.

One day Sequoya decided that he would
figure out a way to do that.
He was just a young man,
who limped when he walked
because he had been sick as a child.
The limp did not keep him from fighting
with the Americans against the English
in the war of 1812.
But he was best at working with his hands.
That was why, when the war was over,
he became a silversmith, making buckles and pins
and other things, out of silver.

In his spare time, he did something else.
He began to make little signs to stand for every word
in the Cherokee language.
Soon he saw that would mean making thousands of signs.
Who could remember so many?

He thought about the problem and then realized
that every word was made up of different sounds.

There were not thousands of different sounds—
just different combinations.
He began to listen carefully to every word he heard.
He broke up each word into its different sounds.
He made a different sign for every sound.

The months went by. The years went by.
Sequoya was married and his wife thought that
he was wasting his time with these marks on birch bark.
But Sequoya kept on.

He had a little daughter, Ahyoka,
and he showed her how the signs on the birch bark
could be read as sounds that made words.
He tested the signs on friends until
they could read the sounds as words.
Finally he had eighty-six marks or signs,
standing for the syllables that made up
the words of the Cherokee language.

Sequoya and his family, and some other Cherokees,
moved west from Tennessee into Arkansas,
and Sequoya had another chance to test
his "talking leaves."

He wrote letters about the move
to friends in Tennessee.
They read the letters easily and told their friends
the news they had brought.

Word of these letters came to the Cherokee chiefs.
They called a council to find out about this new magic.
Sequoya came and brought his daughter, Ahyoka.
Ahyoka was taken a long way from her father
and the chiefs.
She could not hear anything they said.
The chiefs spoke and Sequoya made his signs on paper
to stand for the sounds of their words.
Someone went to fetch Ahyoka.
Ahyoka looked at the signs on the paper
and repeated every word the chiefs had said
when she could not hear them.

The chiefs were astonished.
They tested Ahyoka again and again.
Finally, they said,
"Teach us to do that.
Teach us to read the marks and make them."

The chiefs went home from the meeting and
spread the word of the new writing from village to village.
Sequoya and his daughter went home to Arkansas,
but the miracle had happened.
Soon almost everyone in the Cherokee nation had learned
to read and write the Cherokee language.

Before long, the Cherokee chiefs were writing down
a Constitution for their people,
very like the Constitution of the United States.
They began a newspaper to print the news in Cherokee.

All of this did not help the Cherokees at all
when white men discovered gold on their lands in Georgia.
Gold!
The promise of gold had brought white men to America
in the beginning
and led them to many cruel deeds.

Now they broke a long promise to the Cherokees
that their land in Tennessee and Georgia
was to be theirs forever.
They said the Cherokees must leave that land

and move far west, to Oklahoma.
Finally, they sent soldiers to force the Cherokees
to leave their farms, their homes, their belongings.
Ever afterwards, the Cherokees called
the long, hard, hungry journey they had to make
"The Trail of Tears."

But Sequoya and his family had already
moved to Oklahoma.
Sequoya was there to welcome his people when they came.
His patience and kindness helped them
settle in their new home.

And Sequoya himself was honored by everyone,
even the white men who treated his people so badly.
Their alphabet had grown over the centuries.
Sequoya had invented a sort of alphabet
or syllabary—because it had signs for syllables—
in the course of twelve years.
Towns and countries were named for Sequoya.
Even the great redwood trees of California
were named Sequoya trees, in honor of this man,
who had invented a written language for his people.

CRAZY HORSE...
and Custer's
Last Stand

Wagon trains, filled with white families,
were going farther west,
across the plains, across the mountains,
to California.
Gold had been discovered there,
and gold had always drawn the white men.

And now as the wagon trains came,
white men built forts along the trail
and soldiers came to man them.
Agents came from the government in Washington

to buy Indian land with gifts and promises.
They promised food throughout the year
if the Indians would stay away from the trail.
They promised that white men
would never bother the Indians
if they stayed on the lands they were not selling.

And so some of the chiefs of the Sioux and the Cheyenne,
whose homeland this was,
put their names to the treaties,
and led their people back into the hills
away from the trail.

Then the troubles started.
White men killed the buffalo along the trail
by the hundreds and thousands.
They took the hides and left the flesh to rot.
They were destroying the food that the Indians counted on
through the long winters.

There were other troubles.
The white men did not keep their promise
to provide the Indians with other food through the winter.

100

They did not keep their promise to
leave the Indians alone in the lands reserved for them.
Why?
Gold.
Gold had been found on Indian land in Montana,
and the white men streamed in to look for it.

Around the campfires in the Sioux and Cheyenne villages
the Indians could not talk of anything except
what to do about the white men.
Some were so angry that they wanted to attack white people
wherever they saw them.
But there were chiefs who knew that this
would only bring more trouble.
They tried to make plans.

Crazy Horse was a chief of a Sioux tribe
called the Oglala.
He was young and brave and reckless,
but he knew his people would have a much better chance
against the white men
if they joined with other Sioux tribes.
He powwowed with a chief of the Hunkpapa Sioux,

Sitting Bull,

and with the chiefs of other Sioux tribes also.

They decided to bring all their tribes together

in a valley in Montana

by the banks of the Little Big Horn River.

There they would decide what to do.

Off in their forts, the white men heard

that the Indians were gathering,

but they were not much alarmed.

They were sure they could defeat any group of Indians.

Colonel George Custer was chosen

to lead a war party against the Indians

who had gathered around Crazy Horse and Sitting Bull.

Custer set out with seven hundred men

and rode boldly up the Montana canyons.

As he rode, he planned his attack.

One group of his men would circle the Indian camp

while three other groups would attack from the front.

Fearlessly, Custer and his men

rode up the valley to the Indian camp

on the Little Big Horn.

103

They had no idea that
five thousand Sioux and Cheyenne warriors
were waiting for them,
waiting to swoop down from every direction.

Sitting Bull stood on a hill, chanting a war song
and praying to the Great Spirit for good fortune in battle.
Crazy Horse led the Indians
as they rode to surprise the white men.
"It's a good day to fight," he called to the warriors.
"It's a good day to die!"
And on they came,
whooping, yelling, shooting guns and arrows both,
taking revenge for years and years
of insults and broken promises.

The battle did not last long.
When it was over, Custer and all of his soldiers
had been killed.

"Custer's Last Stand," the white people called it
when they heard of the defeat.
They called the battle an Indian massacre

and could not wait to revenge themselves
on the Indians who had caused it.

The Indians felt differently about it, of course.
They celebrated their great victory
all that night and the next day.

But they knew more white soldiers would soon
be coming after them.
Sitting Bull took off with his people to Canada.
Crazy Horse led his people to what he hoped was
safer country.
But now the white men came by the thousands
to hunt down Crazy Horse, Sitting Bull, and their people.

Soon Crazy Horse was captured.
Later, by an accident, he was killed at the prison.
Sitting Bull held out in Canada as long as he could,
but his people were starving.
At last he had to surrender to the whites.

The battle at the Little Big Horn River had really been
the Sioux' Last Stand.

STRANGERS
NO MORE

The years went on,
and white men kept coming west
as if there were no end to their numbers.
All the other tribes that lived westward
toward the coast
were defeated in their turn.
There were more battles,
more Indian heroes.
There was Chief Joseph of the Nez Perce,
who tried to lead his people to safety in Canada,
and *almost* did so.

There was Geronimo, an Apache,
who fought and fought and fought again,
until at last, worn out, he surrendered.

Finally, there was no more fighting
between Indian and white men.
The Indians lived on the reservations
that the white men set aside for them.
They could hunt no more, and roam no more
over the land that had once been theirs.

They had to rely on the promises of the white men
for almost everything.
And the white men were no better at keeping promises
than they had ever been.
For the Indians it was a hard and terrible life.
But they did not die out.
They did not disappear.
They had a strength of their own.

And gradually, white men began to see that
the Indians had a wisdom of their own also.
Through the centuries, the Indians had learned

to live with the land,
as white men had not.
They did not take more from the land than they needed.
The land was their "good mother,"
and they did not harm it.

Today, as many Indians follow the ways of white men
and move in the white man's world,
white people are trying at last to learn
from the ways of the Indians,
who knew some things better than they did.

In the beginning, Indians had faced strangers.
The strangers had found the Indians strange too.
Perhaps, one day, neither will be so strange to the other
and both will be happier for it.

THE AUTHOR

JOHANNA JOHNSTON'S writing talent ranges from adult biographies to books for the very young. A particular interest in bringing to life great figures of the past and a broad knowledge of American history have led to many of her titles, including *Together in America, The Challenge and the Answer, A Special Bravery, Thomas Jefferson, His Many Talents,* and *Paul Cuffee, America's First Black Captain.*

For several years Miss Johnston wrote for radio, specializing in programs for children. Among her books for the picture book age are *Edie Changes Her Mind* and the ever-popular *Sugarplum.*

Johanna Johnston was born and educated in Chicago, Illinois, and now lives and works in New York City. She is married and has one daughter.

THE ILLUSTRATOR

ROCCO NEGRI was born in Italy and raised in Argentina. He studied visual arts in New York City and specializes in woodcuts. His illustrations have appeared in magazines and both adult and children's books. His work has been exhibited in the New York area, winning a number of awards.

Mr. Negri lives with his wife and two young sons in Ridgewood, New York, on Long Island.

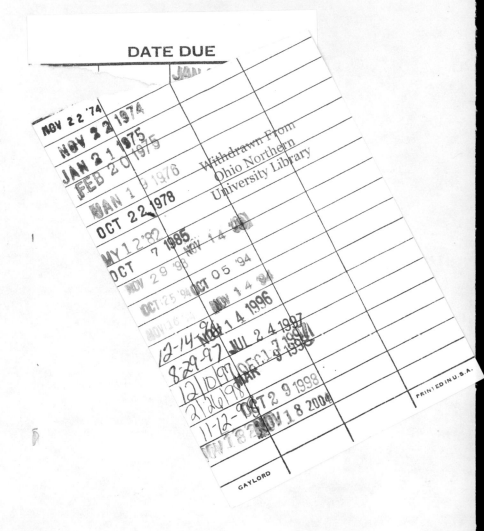